Dino-Mummy

Mark Sperring

Illustrated by Sam Lloyd

BLOOMSBURY

LONDON NEW DELHI NEW YORK SYDNEY

Do you know a secret?
I'm sure you dino-do!

It's something rather special
about a certain "you know who!"

From the moment that you wake up
she's a sing-song superstar,
singing out,

"Good Morning!"

At breakfast, she's amazing —
watch the toast fly through the air!

She's a
dino-conjure-upper . . .

As if that wasn't fab enough,

of course there's dino-more...

She's a kiss-it-better doctor
when she hears your dino-roar.

And the bravest dino-trooper . . .
fighting

dust

and grease

and grime.

She can be your rocket launcher.
HURRAH! What dino-fun!

And when it's time
for dress-up –

can you believe your eyes?

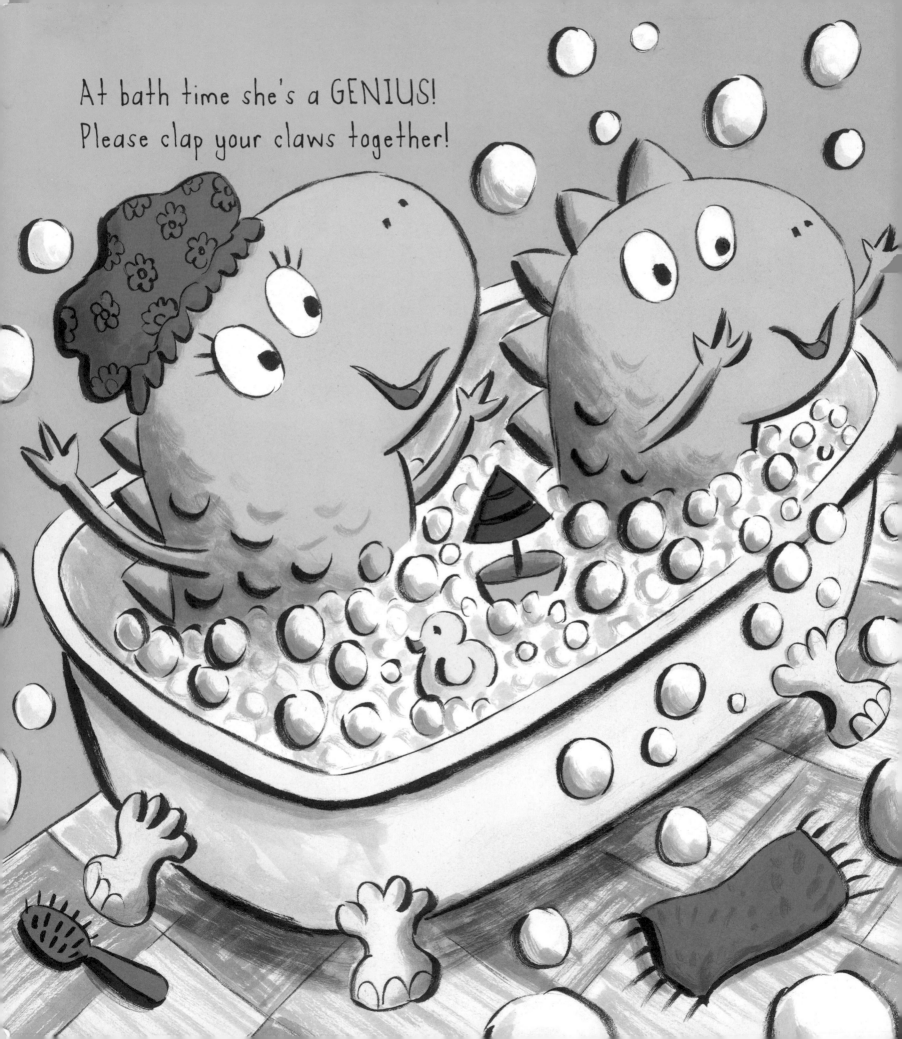

At bath time she's a GENIUS!
Please clap your claws together!

In fact, there is no secret.
It's as clear as dino-day,
from the moment
that you wake up . . .

well, she's great in

So when dino-bedtime comes around,
and you're tucked up oh sooo snuggly,
there's only one thing left to say . . .

For Dino-Mummies everywhere ~ MS

For my sisters Becky and Jess, and all the
other dino-mummies out there ~ SL

Bloomsbury Publishing, London, New Delhi, New York and Sydney
First published in Great Britain in 2014 by Bloomsbury Publishing Plc
50 Bedford Square, London, WC1B 3DP

A CIP catalogue record of this book is available from the British Library

ISBN 978 1 4088 4583 7 (HB)
ISBN 978 1 4088 4584 4 (PB)
ISBN 978 1 4088 4585 1 (eBook)

1 3 5 7 9 10 8 6 4 2

Printed in China by C&C Offset Printing Co Ltd, Shenzhen, Guangdong

www.bloomsbury.com

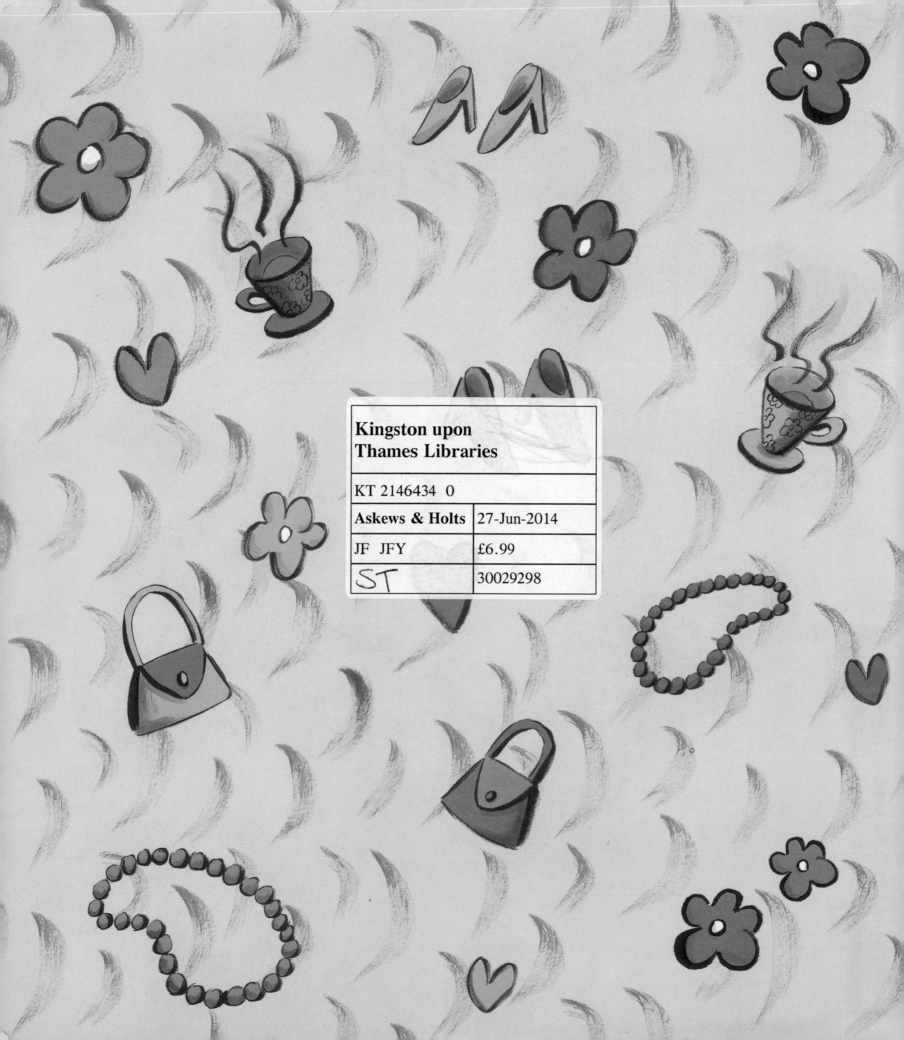